CLASSIC TALES OF
RUPERT

ALFRED BESTALL

HERITAGE

EGMONT

HERITAGE

EGMONT

First published in Great Britain 2012
by Egmont UK Limited
The Yellow Building, 1 Nicholas Road, London W11 4AN
www.egmont.co.uk

ISBN 978 1 4052 6422 8

1 3 5 7 9 10 8 6 4 2

A CIP catalogue record for this title is available from the British Library

Printed and bound in Italy

51106/1

EGMONT LUCKY COIN

Our story began over a century ago, when seventeen-year-old
Egmont Harald Petersen found a coin in the street.

He was on his way to buy a flyswatter, a small hand-operated
printing machine that he then set up in his tiny apartment.

The coin brought him such good luck that today Egmont has
offices in over 30 countries around the world. And that lucky
coin is still kept at the company's head offices in Denmark.

FOREWORD

Rupert Bear is one of the most cherished characters in all of children's literature. Created by Mary Tourtel for the Daily Express newspaper in 1920, the child-like bear and his tales of adventure became extremely popular with children's and adults alike. Yet Rupert was destined for still greater things- in the hands of illustrator Alfred Bestall.

Bestall was born in Burma in 1892, and later studied at Birmingham Central School of Art. He served as a lorry driver in France during World War I, and after the war returned home to a career as a full-time illustrator, including working on Punch magazine and illustrating texts by A. A. Milne and Enid Blyton. His great love was the countryside- he had a house in Beddgellert in Snowdonia- and it is often said that this location fired his imagination. The beautiful mountains and lakes of North Wales were later to inspire his beautiful Rupert endpapers, full of magic and wonder.

He was the writer and illustrator for Rupert for thirty years, and was the creator of the stories in the first ever annual in 1936. It was these annuals that brought Rupert to an even wider audience, and the opportunity to write complete stories for the annuals spurred Bestall on to new creative heights.

Many of Bestall's stories are grounded in a nostalgic, unspoilt landscape, where Rupert and his chums can play happily and have adventures without a care in the world. Yet Bestall could create great flights of fancy too- both the stories in this volume begin in the rural simplicity of Rupert's hometown of Nutwood before journeying to more fantastical, fairytale-like locations.

Alfred Bestall retired as the regular illustrator of Rupert in the Daily Express in 1965, though he continued to contribute to the Rupert annuals until 1973. His Rupert is considered the definitive version of the character, setting the gold standard in terms of artwork and storytelling. His admirers include HRH The Prince of Wales and Paul McCartney.

Bestall was appointed an MBE in 1985 and died peacefully near Porthmadog in North Wales in 1986, aged 93. His legacy is a wealth of timeless, magical storytelling, which will forever in his beautiful illustrations.

CONTENTS

RUPERT
AND THE MARE'S NEST

How Rupert's
kindness to birds was
rewarded by a holiday
at the seaside.

Summer is beginning and a cool bright day has arrived, the sort of day that makes little bears want to skip about and climb trees, so Rupert, after getting his scarf and asking permission of Mrs. Bear, scampers off in search of adventure.

It is a lovely sunny day,
And Rupert hurries out to play.

He hurries in the direction of the Common and soon spies two small figures running towards a stretch of woodland. "I do believe they are Freddy and Ferdy Fox," he murmurs. "What are they up to?"

He meets no friends until, at last,
He sees the Foxes, running fast.

"Do wait for me," calls Rupert, "please!
I want to go and climb some trees."

Running down the hill and across to the wood, Rupert calls out to them and they wait for him. "It's a topping day," cries the little bear. "Let's climb some trees." "Yes, that's what we're going to do," says Freddy. "Come with us. We're going birds' nesting. Look, we've got a basket to carry home the eggs."

But Rupert steps back. "I love climbing trees," he says. "But why rob the nests? I don't think the birds would care much for that." But the Foxes only laugh at him and move away as if they don't know what he is talking about.

The Foxes say, "We're going too,
But we shall take some birds' eggs too."

Rupert tries hard to persuade the Foxes to change their plans, but they run into the woods and are soon out of sight. When he turns away he is startled by the shrill little bird perched on a twig.

A little bird thanks Rupert Bear,
For grumbling at that greedy pair.

"Good for you, Rupert!" it chirrups. "I heard every word you said when you tried to stop those two robbing nests. Perhaps we can do you a good turn one day."

Now Rupert thinks, "It's strange to me,
I wonder where my pals can be?"

It flies off as quickly as it came and as Rupert can find no other friend on the Common he decides to go home.

So feeling rather lonely there,
He hurries home to Mr. Bear.

Seeing one of his father's books on the ground he flops down and opens it. "Why are grown-up books so queer?" he thinks. Suddenly he spells out a word and jumps up in excitement.

They settle down to read and rest,
Till Rupert sees the words – "Mare's Nest".

11

"Please tell me what it means," he cries,
"There's no such thing," his dad replies.

"Daddy, do tell me," he cries, "what is a Mare's Nest?" To his surprise Mr. Bear, now very comfortably reading his paper in a hammock that he has fastened between two trees, smiles and doesn't answer at once. "What an awkward question," he grins, "goodness knows what you will be asking next." Rupert persists in his question and Mr. Bear sighs.

"A Mare's Nest, did you say?" he smiles. "That's difficult. A Mare's Nest? Well, it's the sort of thing you look for and it's not there!" "You're teasing me, Daddy," laughs Rupert. "It must be there sometimes. It's in this book of yours! But a mare isn't a bird. How can it have a nest?" Mr. Bear gets out of his hammock. "I tell you what," he says.

He smiles, then says, "Bring one to me,
And I will take you to the sea."

12

So Rupert hurries out again,
To find his friends and then explain.

"Suppose you and your pals go and search and if you can find me a Mare's Nest I'll take you away for a whole week's holiday at the seaside." Full of excitement Rupert hurries off again and this time he spies two more of his pals, Algy Pug and Willie Mouse. "I say, chaps," he calls, "have you seen a Mare's Nest. My daddy says he will take me to the seaside if I can show him one, so I must find one!"

"That's silly," says the little mouse, "how can there be such a thing?" and he strolls away. Algy, however, gets an idea and points across to some buildings. As Rupert and Algy cross the fields, Algy explains. "This is where Farmer Green lives," he says. "He may be able to help you."

"I'll help you," Algy says, "let's go
And ask them at the farm below."

13

The pug explains as they draw near,
"I know that Farmer Green lives here."

Sure enough they soon meet the
Farmer and he greets them cheerily.
"We're hunting for a Mare's Nest,"
says Rupert. "And we thought
you'd be certain to tell us where
to find one."

To his amazement both Farmer
Green and his mare burst out
laughing. "Now, young Rupert,"
he grins, "don't you try to catch
me with your tricks." Still smiling
he moves away.

The farmer laughs at their request
To help them find a real Mare's Nest.

A bird warns Rupert with alarm,
"Give up, or you may come to harm."

When the two friends return to the Common a bird flies between them. "We've been following and listening to you," squawks the little creature, "and I'm now warning you to give up this search of yours. It's dangerous."

As the bird flutters away Algy looks glum. "This idea of yours doesn't seem very good, Rupert," he says, "the birds don't want us to go. I do believe Willie was right and that there is no such thing as a Mare's Nest. I'm going home." Leaving the little bear he runs off and disappears.

Then Algy looks a trifle glum,
"I'm going home," he tells his chum.

Rupert stops and thinks. "If there is no such thing as a Mare's Nest why did the bird say that it was dangerous to look for it?" he mutters. "I'm not going to give it up. I know what I'll do. I'll ask the Wise Old Owl."

"Now," Rupert thinks, "I'm worried too,
I'll ask the Wise Owl what to do."

He sets off at full-speed for the forest and meets Horace the hedgehog, but before he can speak the bird appears again and squawks in his face. "Oh dear! I wish you wouldn't follow me about," says Rupert.

He meets the hedgehog, but the bird
Returns, before they speak a word.

The bird is still very excited. "We're very grateful to you for trying to stop those people birds' nesting and we don't want you to get in trouble searching for a Mare's Nest." Rupert makes up his mind. "I want to find the Wise Old Owl," he says. "Then if he tells me to go home I'll go."

The bird has hurried back again,
To warn the bear, but all in vain.

Seeing how determined he is the bird at last flies away and Horace offers to show him where the Owl's tree is. Soon the little bear is climbing through thick leaves and branches towards the secret hollow place where he hopes to find the wisest of all birds.

"I must find Owl," says Rupert, so
The hedgehog shows him where to go.

Rupert pours out his story and the owl gazes at him solemnly. "You wish to know what a Mare's Nest is," he says. "Little bear, there are things that we know but must not tell; that is one of them especially today." Rupert stares. "Why especially today," he asks in disappointment. "I can say no more," replies the wise bird. "Now you run home and forget all about it."

The owl says with a solemn stare,
"I must not tell you, little bear."

Sadly Rupert climbs down the tree. Hearing the sound of running feet he turns as the Fox brothers dash out of the thick bushes.

Poor Rupert sadly turns away,
He'll have to leave it for today.

The Foxes now come dashing by,
"We've seen a dreadful bird," they cry.

"Hullo, have you finished birds' nesting?" he asks. "No, don't stop us," gasps Ferdy. "Right in the middle of the wood we met a fearful great bird. It chased us and we're off." They disappear, and Rupert stares. "There are no great birds here," he thinks.

But as evening comes on there is a whirr of wings and a flock of birds sweeps across the darkening sky and, with a start of surprise, he sees that one of them is an enormous creature.

What can they mean? Then Rupert sees
A huge bird fly above the trees.

19

"Now," Rupert cries, "what's this I've found;
A large disc lying on the ground."

The great flock of birds disappear into the darkness, so Rupert hurries homewards and as he goes something on the ground catches his eye. "It looks like a seal or medal," he says. "Who can have dropped it? I must show this to Daddy." Picking it up he finds it very light.

Mr. Bear greets him cheerily. "Hullo, Rupert," he calls. "Have you found me a Mare's Nest?" "Not yet," laughs Rupert, "but I've brought something else, look." "What on earth is it?" says his father. "There's a picture on it of a bird with a very long beak."

Says Mr. Bear, "What can it be?
Some kind of seal, it seems to me."

While Rupert has some supper Mr. Bear mends the broken chain. "You must take this to Constable Growler in the morning," he says. "He may know where it belongs."

He mends the broken chain with care,
Watched by an eager little bear.

Long after Rupert is in bed Mrs. Bear comes into his room. "The birds are making a terrible noise when they should be asleep," she says. They peer out into the darkness without being able to see anything. "There is certainly something queer going on," thinks Rupert.

That night, the birds make such a din,
That Mrs. Bear comes running in.

Next morning Rupert carefully packs the strange seal and sets off. "Tell Constable Growler just where you found the seal," says Mrs. Bear. "I wish we could keep it," smiles Rupert, "but it looks precious, and the person who dropped it must be worrying about it."

The seal must be returned, and so
To P.C. Growler it must go.

He notices that a blackbird after fluttering round and listening to what he says, flies rapidly towards the wood, but he thinks no more of it until his way is barred by dozens of birds who fly in his face making a great noise.

But Rupert soon has quite a shock,
For birds fly round him in a flock.

It seems just like a horrid dream,
"We think you have our seal," they scream.

"What have you got in that parcel?" they scream. "Show it to us at once." Although he is startled by the crowd of birds Rupert refuses to open the parcel. "I'm sure it's something precious," he says, "and I'm taking it straight to Constable Growler."

Pressing round him more furiously than ever they drive him before them right into the wood where, on a rock and looking very glum, sits the largest bird Rupert has ever seen. "That is the creature that frightened the Foxes!" he gasps. "Oh dear, what shall I do?"

They push him till he sees once more,
The fearsome bird he met before.

He's looking very cross today,
And Rupert wants to run away.

After hearing what has happened the great bird looks very stern. "They tell me that you've found something precious, little bear," he says. "If it is the seal with the picture of my king it belongs to me. It is my royal mark and I must have it this minute. If you disobey me you do so at your peril!"

He glares fiercely but at that instant a little bird flies forward. "Don't hurt him. He is our friend," he calls. "He tried to stop the Foxes from robbing our nests. Speak to him kindly."

A bird flies and says, "Take care!
You must not harm kind Rupert Bear."

24

Rupert does not doubt any longer that what is in the parcel belongs to this bird, so he unfastens the paper. On seeing the royal seal the huge bird swoops down with every sign of joy. Other birds slip it over his head and he proudly returns to his rock.

When Rupert holds the seal on high,
The huge bird gives a joyful cry.

"My daddy mended the chain, but why do you wear it?" Rupert asks. "I am a carrier bird for our king and I wear this seal to show that I belong to him. Without the seal I have no power and I dare not go home."

He proudly wears the seal and chain,
Now he can do his work again.

The birds explain, "You helped our king,
For you we will do anything."

Feeling very happy that everyone is now so friendly Rupert starts home, but he is soon stopped. "Anyone who does a good turn to our king must be rewarded," says the little bird. "By returning our precious seal you have indeed done well. What reward would you like?"

Rupert thinks quickly. "What I really want to see is a Mare's Nest," he says. "The Old Owl and the others birds wouldn't help. Will the carrier show me one?" The bird pauses then tells him to climb on a nearby branch.

"Oh good!" cries Rupert Bear with glee,
"A Mare's Nest I should like to see."

To Rupert's astonishment the great bird moves underneath the branch and tells him to let himself down. "You will be quite safe on my back, little bear," he says. "What you have asked is too difficult for me. Only our king can allow anyone to see a Mare's Nest. We must go and see what he says about it."

The large bird says, "Our king will know.
Climb on my back and off we'll go."

Without delay they soar away strongly over the fields until the sea disappears. Then up they go again until they are lost in the blue and all the land disappears.

The bird sets off upon its flight,
While Rupert holds on, very tight.

They keep on flying very high,
To reach a palace in the sky.

At first Rupert is frightened at being so high in the air and on such an unsafe perch, but he finds the great bird always rights him as he slips. Higher and higher they go until, sweeping over a cloud they see a vast palace beneath them and many birds of strange shapes come to meet them.

A moment later they alight on a marble terrace and Rupert is introduced to the court chamberlain, a very important bird also wearing a seal. After hearing the story of the carrier bird's adventure the court chamberlain turns to Rupert.

The chamberlain comes out to see,
Just who these visitors can be.

"You, little bear, shall now make your bow to the king," he says. "Follow me." And leading the way into the palace he enters a brightly lit apartment, where stands a gorgeous creature clothed in ermine and wearing a crown. "That's the bird whose picture was on the seal," thinks Rupert.

He hears their tale with some surprise,
"I'll take you to our king," he cries.

But he bows low while his story is being repeated. "He shall be well rewarded," says the king. "Come, we shall take a turn on the terrace and he shall tell me his wishes."

The bird king says, "You have done well,
And now your wishes you shall tell."

Out on the terrace Rupert eagerly tells of his search for the Mare's Nest, and at first the king looks rather serious. "You are a strange little bear," he says, "and you are the only person I have met who believes that there is such a thing. It is a secret known only to us birds."

The king says, "I will do my best,
To grant your very strange request."

He walks about in silence for awhile, then calls his penguin attendant to him. "Go and find the court chamberlain and bid him to come to me," he orders.

Two messengers are sent to bring
The chamberlain, to see the king.

The king says, "You may help this bear,
And give him my royal seal to wear."

"I think the matter can be arranged.
This little bear has met with
my favour," says the king to the
chamberlain. "Therefore I have
decided that his strange wish shall
be granted. He shall see the Mare's
Nest. Make sure that he wears a
royal seal for his own safety."

The chamberlain looks surprised,
but he bows to the king and sets off
briskly, leading Rupert to another
part of the palace while the king's
own attendants march with them.
"I knew I was right," says the little
bear. "We shan't be long now!"

The chamberlain cries, "Follow me!"
And Rupert does so, eagerly.

31

They go into an office, where
The secretary meets the bear.

Taking Rupert into a small office the court chamberlain explains his orders. Then the penguin retires and the little bear is left facing a business-like bird wearing large spectacles, who silently hangs a seal round his neck. "I am the king's secretary," he says.

"His orders must be obeyed and this sparrow will guide you to the Mare's Nest. You are in danger, but you are a brave little bear and that seal will keep you safe."

A sparrow is to lead the way,
So off they go, without delay.

The way is up a rocky slope,
But Rupert follows, full of hope.

Leaving the palace by a small door the sparrow leads Rupert down a steep slope of broken rock and tells him to scramble up. At the top, the little bear sees a pile of sticks perched on an isolated pinnacle of rock.

"There you are," says the sparrow in a scared voice. "Now you've seen a Mare's Nest. I'm off, you find your own way back." The bird disappears leaving Rupert all alone. "How can it be a Mare's Nest," thinks the little bear. "No horse could ever get up there!"

"There is the nest!" the sparrow cries;
Then, hurriedly, away he flies.

The quick disappearance of the sparrow puzzles Rupert. "It seemed to be frightened of something," he murmurs. "But why? It's all so quiet up here." However, he notices with anxiety that no other birds are flying anywhere near the nest.

When Rupert tries to climb the rock,
He suddenly has quite a shock.

At that moment the great pile begins to creak and tremble and, to Rupert's astonishment, a horse's head appears wearing a royal seal.

The nest begins to shake about,
And then a horse's head looks out.

34

Almost before Rupert can cry out, the animal rises to its feet, spreads a huge pair of wings and swings into the air. "So it is the Mare's Nest, and it's a flying mare!" gasps the little bear. The graceful creature sweeps towards him.

The mare has wings and takes to flight,
She is a fine and graceful sight.

"What do you mean by disturbing my rest?" she demands fiercely. "Do you not know that none may see and live." Suddenly she spies the royal crest that Rupert is wearing. "I crave your pardon, little brother," she says. "I did not see that you, too, are in the king's favour. What do you want of me?"

She lands and speaks to Rupert Bear,
"I see the royal seal you wear."

Now that he has got over his fright Rupert eagerly pours out his story. "I was searching for a Mare's Nest because my daddy told me to," says Rupert. "But please tell me who you are and why your nest is so secret?" "You may as well know," says the flying mare.

*"I am the king's royal charger, and
I carry him about his land."*

"I am the king's charger. When he visits his realm he cannot fly because he wears his ermine robes, so I carry him. Now farewell. I must tell you no more." She soars into the sky, while Rupert carefully starts back on his long journey to the palace.

*"Oh, thank you!" Rupert cries, "and now
I must climb down these rocks, somehow."*

Near the bottom of the slope several birds fly towards Rupert. "Good gracious, are you still alive?" cries the first one. "I'm wearing the king's seal so that kept me safe," says the little bear. "It was a wonderful sight up there," and he starts to explain how his father started him off on his adventure.

When Rupert comes, the birds fly round,
Surprised to see him safe and sound.

Then he suddenly pauses. "Oh dear, I haven't finished my work yet!" he gasps. "However can I do the rest of it?"

The little bear stands still and sighs,
"I've thought of something else," he cries.

Seeing Rupert's worried expression one of the guards asks Rupert what is the matter. "My daddy says there is no such thing as a Mare's Nest," says the little bear. "And he promised to take me for a week to the seaside if I can show him one. Well now I've seen one, but how on earth am I going to show him one?"

"I saw that Mare's Nest, thanks to you;
But can my daddy see it too?"

"Quite impossible, quite, quite impossible," says the guard importantly. "Come with me. It's high time you said goodbye to the king and started for home."

"Impossible," the guards reply,
"And now you'll have to say goodbye."

So Rupert hurries to the king,
To give him thanks for everything.

On reaching the king, Rupert gives him back the royal seal and tells him how safe it has kept him during his adventure. Then he explains what is worrying him. At first the king is speechless, then, at length, he smiles.

"Well, I like people who are not afraid to ask for big things," he says. "Let's see what we can do." Calling the guard, he cries, "Go to the mountains and bid my charger come to me here. I have work for her."

The king hears Rupert's further plea,
Says, "Bring my charger here to me."

He orders fruit for Rupert Bear,
While they await the flying mare.

The king laughed and ordered fine fruits to be brought. "You will not be with us much longer, little bear," he says, "but you shall not go home hungry."

During the meal the flying mare appears and alights on the terrace and bows low to the king. "I am ready," she says. "Tell me your wishes and I will fly to do them." With growing excitement Rupert listens to the unfolding of his plans.

She soon appears and bows down low,
Then says, "Your wishes I would know."

*The king explains, "This scroll will tell
The Nutwood birds they pleased me well."*

"The carrier bird who brought you also brought good account of the birds of Nutwood," says the king. "They are doing their work so well that I have decided to give them a royal scroll to show my pleasure, but the carrier bird shall not take it for me this time.

"Here it is sealed and finished and you, little bear, shall take it for me, and my charger will fly you and tell you the rest of the plans." "How perfectly topping!" cries Rupert, jumping with excitement. "When shall we be off? Can we start now?"

*Now Rupert is to ride the mare,
And give the scroll when he is there.*

41

The mare continues with the flight,
And will not land while it is light.

The flying mare kneels so that Rupert can take his seat on her back. The next moment they are soaring high in the air, but to Rupert's surprise they spend time soaring round in circles.

"Aren't we going to land?" he asks. "Not till night falls," replies the other. "I may not visit your land by daylight. That is not allowed." But when darkness falls she sets a straight course and glides down and down until she lands on top of a pine tree.

When darkness falls, she lands with ease
Upon the highest of the trees.

"You are near Nutwood Common," says the mare. "This tree is easy to climb down. The messenger of the birds will meet you and you can give him this royal scroll, then go straight to your home." "But how about showing my daddy a Mare's Nest?" asks Rupert.

Poor Rupert wears a worried frown,
He wishes he were safely down.

"You will be fetched when we are ready for you," replies the mare. The pale moon gives a little light as Rupert feels his way downwards. Suddenly he notices a dark shape floating silently round and round him.

As he gets nearer to the ground,
He sees a dark shape flying round.

The dark shape settles on the tree,
"It's Wise Owl!" Rupert shouts with glee.

Before Rupert reaches the ground the dark shape settles on a branch beside him. "Why it's the Wise Old Owl!" gasps the little bear. "Of course you are the bird that flies by night; you must be the messenger I am expecting. Look, here is the royal scroll that your king sent for all the birds of Nutwood."

"That is indeed an honour," says the owl proudly. "I saw you arrive on the king's charger. I must go to her now for orders." As Rupert reaches the edge of the wood a large shape looms up before him.

He is the messenger all right,
And takes the scroll with great delight.

44

"Constable Growler," he cries happily. "Oh how glad I am to see you. It's terribly lonely in there." "And I'm glad to see you, young Rupert," says the constable. "Half the village has been searching for you for many hours."

Now P.C. Growler comes along,
And asks young Rupert what is wrong.

Rupert prattles away as they make their way back to Nutwood, but the policeman cannot make head nor tail of his adventures. "Mare's Nests and such are not in my line," he says gruffly. Soon Rupert is running to meet Mr. and Mrs. Bear in his cottage.

He takes him home, as it is late,
And there his parents sadly wait.

How glad they are to see him well,
And hear the tale he has to tell.

Rupert is so excited at his adventure that he starts telling his story as soon as he gets into the cottage and though Mrs. Bear gets his supper he still goes on. "You promised to take me to the seaside if I showed you a Mare's Nest, didn't you, Daddy?" he cries.

"Well, I've seen one, I'll show you one too, later, when we are fetched tonight." Mrs. Bear stares. "No more outings tonight," she says. "It's long past your bedtime, so off you go. The whole thing sounds like a fairy tale to me."

Says Mrs. Bear, "It's time for bed,
Be off with you, you sleepy head."

Rupert undresses very slowly
and while he has his bath and
prepares for bed he thinks about
his adventure. Just as he is getting
between the sheets a sharp noise
makes him start.

A sound now reaches Rupert's ear,
Perhaps the messenger is here?

The next moment he is out of the
room and searching for his father.
"Daddy, Daddy," he calls, "I told
you that we should be fetched
tonight, and somebody's tapping
at my window." "Good gracious,
why aren't you asleep hours ago?"
grumbles Mr. Bear. "I suppose I'd
better come."

He hurries down the stairs again,
To find his father and explain.

47

Mr. Bear pulls back Rupert's curtains and opens the window. Next moment a silent shape glides towards the light and settles on the sill. "Look, look!" cries Rupert. "It's the Wise Old Owl.

"It is the owl!" he cries with glee,
"And now the Mare's Nest you shall see."

"He's the messenger and he must have come for us to go and see the Mare's Nest. Do let's go straight away!" The owl doesn't say a word but gazes steadily at Mr. Bear. Then, with a loud hoot, it glides back into the night.

Says Mr. Bear, "It's late, you know;
But still, to please you, I will go."

Poor Mrs. Bear is worried too,
When told what they propose to do.

"Well this beats me," says Mr. Bear. "You said we should be called and I suppose we'd better go, though what your mother will say I can't imagine." Mrs. Bear is horrified at Rupert going out again so late, but when she hears the full story she sighs and then wraps warm shawls around Rupert, putting his dressing gown over them.

Soon the little bear is perched on his father's shoulder, and the owl, who has waited for them, leads the way in the moonlight through the forest.

They find the Wise Old Owl outside,
He's waiting there to be their guide.

In the middle of the forest Rupert stops and points. "There you are, Daddy," he cries. "That tall tree! D'you see it? There's a great pile of sticks and branches right at the top of it and now I've shown you a Mare's Nest!" "How do I know it's a Mare's Nest?" murmurs Mr. Bear, staring hard. As he speaks a great creature rises from it and, standing black against the sky, it spreads its wings.

He leads them straight back to the tree,
The Mare's Nest is quite plain to see.

Then it soars away and is lost to sight. The next moment the owl is beside them, ready to lead them both home again.

The mare flies off, as they stand there;
"How wonderful!" gasps Mr. Bear.

Next morning Mr. Bear is sure,
He dreamed it all the night before.

After the excitement of the night Mrs. Bear brings Rupert his breakfast in bed and his father sits by him. "That Mare's Nest was the most wonderful thing," says Mr. Bear. "So wonderful that I'm not sure that we weren't dreaming or whether we really saw it."

When he is dressed Rupert insists on going to the forest. Before long they stop and gaze around. "I can't make out where the owl led us," says Mr. Bear. "Everything looks quite different this morning."

So, after breakfast, back they go,
But now, the place they do not know.

51

Rupert and his father search but can find no trace of the track that they followed in the middle of the night. "I'm beginning to think we were dreaming," says Mr. Bear. "We'd better go home again."

They search around, but all in vain,
They cannot find the nest again.

Just as they are leaving the wood, a loud chirrup interrupts them. "Just a minute, Rupert," pipes the little creature. "You did us a good turn once when you tried to stop those foxes. Now perhaps I can do one for you."

A tiny bird to Rupert flies,
"I'll help you if you like," he cries.

The little bird has heard all about Rupert's disappointment and offers to guide them to where they want to go. In great excitement Rupert takes his father's hand and drags him back to follow their leader.

In great excitement, off they run,
"What luck!" laughs Rupert. "This is fun."

At length Mr. Bear stops and points. "That's it!" he cries. "That's the tree we saw last night, but, look, there's no sign of the Mare's Nest. We must have been dreaming after all!" Rupert stares in bewilderment, but the little bird whispers, "Go nearer to the tree."

But when they find the tree – oh dear,
The nest has disappeared, I fear.

Now when they start to look around,
The nest is scattered on the ground.

Following the advice of the little
bird, Rupert and his father go nearer
the tree and all round the foot
of it they see a ring of sticks and
branches of all shapes and sizes.

Mr. Bear looks closely at them. "This
is a pine tree," he says, "but these
are not pine branches. They must
have been brought here." Here the
bird joins in. "You're quite right,"
it pipes. "No one has ever seen a
Mare's Nest. The mare always kicks
them to pieces before daybreak."

The bird explains, "That's all you'll find.
She never leaves her nest behind."

Now Mr. Bear says, "I agree,
You've earned your visit to the sea."

Rupert and his father start homewards. "Remember," chirrups the little bird, "if ever you see a tree surrounded by branches that don't belong, it's a sure sign that a Mare's Nest has been there the night before."

"Well," says Mr. Bear in astonishment, "you have done what I thought nobody could do, Rupert. You have shown me a Mare's Nest, and now I'll carry out my promise and we'll have a jolly week at the seaside." And they go straight to the station to find out the times of the trains to Rocky Bay.

They go to ask, that very day,
About the trains to Rocky Bay.

RUPERT

and the

LOST CUCKOO

It is one of the busiest birds in Nutwood Village, and how Rupert misses its cheery voice! After a long search he discovers why it has vanished from its usual home.

One morning in August, Rupert is walking on the Common when he hears an unusual noise. "This place is always quiet," he thinks. "I wonder what is happening." Climbing a low bank he spies a group of birds fluttering and chattering excitedly.

Says Rupert, "What a noisy crowd!
I can't think why they chirp so loud!"

At the sight of him they fly away and, as he hurries forward, Rupert sees them join a larger flight high in the sky. "Different kinds of birds don't generally fly together like that," he murmurs. "Something is happening. What can the excitement be?"

Though Rupert wishes they would stay,
The birds are scared, and fly away.

"One bird has turned – I wonder why,"
Says Rupert, gazing at the sky.

As Rupert watches the sky, one of the birds separates itself from the flight and glides downwards. Something odd about its shape makes him gaze at it intently as it settles on a distant fence.

Creeping round the bushes inquisitively on tiptoe, he manages to get quite near without disturbing it. "Why, surely it's a wooden bird!" he gasps. In his surprise he moves a branch, startling the queer creature which flaps creakily away in the direction of the village.

A closer view makes Rupert blink,
Says he, "It's made of wood, I think!"

He tries to keep the bird in sight,
But soon it vanishes in flight.

Hurrying forward to keep the stranger in sight, Rupert meets his pals Rastus and Lily Duckling, but they haven't noticed it and don't seem very interested, so he scampers home.

"Guess what I've seen, Mummy," he cries, "a live wooden bird, a real one. It flew this way and it was carrying a spray of leaves in its beak. What d'you think it can be?"

Puffs Rupert, breathless from his run,
"I've seen a bird – a wooden one!"

"Yes," Rupert nods, "I'm sure it's true,
Its wings were creaking as it flew!"

"You must be dreaming," smiles Mrs. Bear, who is busy preparing dinner. "Are you sure you haven't been sleeping out on the Common?" Rupert gets very excited as he continues his story. "I really did see a wooden bird," he insists. "It came this way and its wings creaked as it flew." Mrs. Bear looks thoughtful. "Did you say it creaked?" she murmurs.

"I heard a curious creaking noise in this very cottage not long ago. I wonder . . ." Leading the way past the cuckoo clock in the hall she looks in the other rooms. The windows are open, but there is no sign of any stranger in the house, and all is quiet.

Says Mrs. Bear, "That's rather queer,
For I've heard creaking noises here."

A thorough search of the cottage reveals nothing out of order and at length Mrs. Bear sends Rupert out again. "There should be plenty of blackberries about now," she says. "Will you pick me a nice basketful?"

"The blackberries are nice and sweet,
So will you pick us some to eat?"

So away he races back to the Common. "Hullo, there's another flight of birds," he exclaims. "And one of them is a very odd shape. It's not a bit like that wooden bird. I wonder what it can be. And where are they going? They seem to be heading for the lake." There is no shortage of blackberries, and Rupert is soon busy.

"Those birds are heading for the lake,"
Says Rupert. "What a noise they make!"

Asks Rupert, "Did you see them pass?"
As Horace shuffles through the grass.

Before he has filled the basket there is a gentle snuffling noise and Horace the hedgehog appears. "Hullo, you're just the person to explain what is happening," cries the little bear. "I've seen such strange birds. They were . . ."

"Talking of birds, there is something queer going on," Horace interrupts. "Can you hear what I can hear?" Rupert listens, and from behind him comes the call of the cuckoo, small but clear.

Then Horace hears a funny sound,
So Rupert stops and looks around.

63

*"In August cuckoos shouldn't call,
They ought not to be here at all!"*

Rupert cannot understand what Horace means. "But a cuckoo isn't queer," he says. "There are lots of them. Now these other birds I've been telling you about, they're queer. One was made of wood, and now . . ." But Horace interrupts again. "There aren't lots of cuckoos any more. Don't you know your poetry? It's August now and they've all gone. The one we heard was late."

Grumpily he disappears and Rupert, meeting Lily Duckling, asks if she has seen the wooden bird again.

*Says Lily, "We've not seen or heard
A creature like that wooden bird."*

Back to his cottage Rupert goes,
It's time to have a meal, he knows.

Neither Lily nor Rastus has seen any more of the wooden bird so Rupert, realising that he is hungry, hurries home, where he finds Mrs. Bear in the kitchen.

"Will dinner be ready soon, Mummy?" he asks. "All in good time," she smiles. "I'll bring it in sharp at one o'clock. I'm waiting for the clock to strike!" "But it's past one o'clock," cries Rupert. "I looked as I came through the hall." "Surely it can't be," says Mrs. Bear. "I've listened carefully and it hasn't struck yet."

Smiles Mummy, "Dinner isn't late,
The clock's not struck – you'll have to wait."

*And then they hurry to the hall
To see the clock upon the wall.*

Rupert is so certain of himself that Mrs. Bear, feeling very mystified, follows him into the hall. "You're quite right!" she says as she gazes at the cuckoo clock. "It's well past one o'clock, but I'm quite sure it didn't strike one. There must be something wrong with the works."

But Rupert gets a sudden idea and fetching a chair he opens the little door at the top. "No wonder it wouldn't strike," he calls anxiously. "Do you see what has happened? Our cuckoo has gone!" Rupert and his mummy are bewildered.

*But Rupert, standing on a chair,
Can see the cuckoo isn't there.*

"Our cuckoo might be lost, you know.
I heard one call not long ago."

"A cuckoo clock isn't much use without its little bird," says Mrs. Bear. "Oh dear," moans Rupert. "I heard a cuckoo when I was on the Common just now. It had a little voice, too. D'you think it could have been our cuckoo? If so I think I know which way it went. May I go and search?"

After dinner he starts and at once he spies a group of his pals, the Rabbit twins, Bill Badger and Willie Mouse, all standing and talking earnestly.

"My pals look serious today,
And seem to have a lot to say."

Rupert runs up to his friends. "I say, listen," he calls. "All sorts of queer things are happening! This morning I saw a wooden bird, then I saw another larger bird with a huge tail, and now, guess what! – the cuckoo out of my cuckoo clock has vanished!"

"There's something puzzling all of you."
Says Rupert. "So please tell me too."

Bill gives him an odd look. "Now I'll show you a queer thing," he says. "D'you notice anything missing from the Squire's house over there?" Rupert stares. "Why, yes," he gasps. "The weathercock has gone too!"

"What's happened to the weathercock?"
Bill asks. "It gives us quite a shock."

All the little pals are excited at the disappearance of the Squire's weathercock and they scamper off to fetch Constable Growler. "Ay, 'tis gone. It must have fell down like," he says gravely. "Come, we'll tell the Squire and then you shall help me to look for it."

Old Growler looks up with a frown,
And thinks the thing has fallen down.

But Rupert stays behind. "That bird with the big tail that I saw," he mutters. "It was just the shape of a weathercock. Oh dear, what does it mean? First the wooden bird, then my cuckoo – and now this! Something strange is happening."

Soon Rupert's left to puzzle out
Just what the mystery's about.

69

Although the birds hear Rupert's call,
They do not answer him at all.

None of Rupert's friends seems to be able to explain anything, so he determines to try by himself to find out why such mysterious things have been happening. He calls out to some birds that he sees returning from the lake, but they do not stop to answer him.

At length he finds one resting on a branch. "Do please tell me," he begs. "What are the birds doing today? I saw a wooden one this morning and now the cuckoo from my cuckoo clock and the Squire's weathercock have gone!" At first the bird does not answer.

"Ah, there's a bird perched on a tree!
Perhaps he will explain to me."

Then it looks rather annoyed. "You're not very clever," it squawks. "Surely you knew that that wooden bird was the dove out of Mr. Noah's Ark!" "Why, of course it must have been!" cries Rupert. "But what was . . ."

"That's Noah's dove – do use your eyes!"
The angry little bird replies.

"Don't ask any more silly questions!" screams the other. "That's all you need to know, isn't it?" And it flies away out of sight, leaving the little bear puzzled at the bird's annoyance and feeling even more mystified.

The little bear is at a loss
To know what's made the bird so cross.

Then Rupert gazes from the hill
To where the lake lies calm and still.

Rupert waits and ponders what the bird has said. "It sounds as if the wooden bird is the key to the mystery and if I could find it I could also find my cuckoo," he says. "That means I must find Mr. Noah. If he is in the district he must have water to float his Ark in, and the only water quiet enough is the Nutwood Lake."

He hurries up the hill until he can see the lake far below and soon he is thrusting through a thick wood on his way down. Rupert breathes with relief after he has struggled through the wood. As he pauses to get his bearings he gives a sudden start, for there, right beside him, is the wooden dove itself, standing on a branch and watching him intently.

So through the woodland, thick and dark,
He makes his way to Noah's Ark.

The dove, a twig held in its beak,
Frowns at the bear, but will not speak.

"Why, you're the very person I'm looking for," cries the little bear. "Please, do you know where my cuckoo is?" For a moment the dove, still holding a leaf in its beak, eyes him silently.

Then, without a single word, it flies rapidly away towards the lake. "Oh dear, I'm not getting very much help," sighs Rupert.

Then suddenly with wings outspread,
It flies towards the lake ahead.

73

"Do you belong to Noah too?
If so, I'd like to speak to you."

"Please, do you know if my little cuckoo came this way?" The animals look very grave. "Have you had an invitation?" asks the giraffe. Rupert is taken aback. "Invitation to what?" he says. "I don't understand. I only want my cuckoo!"

Pressing onwards to the lake, Rupert finds his way barred by two large toy animals, an elephant and a giraffe, who are quickly joined by a wooden tiger. They all regard him with silent disapproval. "Are you all from the Ark?" asks Rupert.

"Please, did my cuckoo come this way?"
Asks Rupert, but they will not say.

The small giraffe speaks for the rest
And says, "Are you another guest?"

While Rupert has been speaking, several more animals have appeared and now, without answering him, they move a little distance away and stand in a solemn circle. "I wish I could hear what they are saying," murmurs Rupert. "They don't seem a bit pleased to see me."

He sits down to wait and at length most of the others hurry away to the lake, leaving one who approaches Rupert. "We have decided to ask our Captain about you," it says, "so you'd better follow me. Come along."

The animals walk on again,
But one moves closer to explain.

"I'll find my cuckoo soon, I hope,"
Thinks Rupert, running down the slope.

Still feeling very bewildered Rupert follows his small leader down the last slopes of the hill. At the edge of the lake he is confronted by a little old man who looks at him gravely.

"Oh, please, are you Mr. Noah?" he says breathlessly. "Yes, I am," says the little man. "And you're Rupert, aren't you? My animals told me about you. Well, your cuckoo is quite safe, so now you can go home again." "But why did it go away?" cries Rupert. "Our clock's no good without it."

He meets a man who's white and old,
"Yes, I am Noah," he is told.

Says Rupert, "But our clock's no good
Without a cuckoo made of wood."

As soon as he has spoken Mr. Noah begins to walk away, but Rupert is not satisfied. "If you know where my cuckoo is won't you let me see it?" he pleads. "Has it gone for ever? Surely you don't want it for the Ark, do you?"

Mr. Noah turns and looks at him more kindly. "Dear me, how anxious you are," he says. "I invited your cuckoo to come here for the day, but I didn't invite you. That's why my animals want to stop you. Come, I'll tell you all about it."

"I cannot see my cuckoo – why?"
Asks Rupert with an anxious sigh.

"Tired birds," says Noah, "come to stay
When they have earned a holiday."

While Rupert listens Mr. Noah explains the mystery. "Every year I arrange a special picnic," he says. "And I only invite those who need it most.

"When my messenger went to Nutwood he decided that your cuckoo and the Squire's weathercock were the hardest- worked creatures in the village, so we asked them here for a day's outing and a trip on the Ark. See, there it is, just returning."

"Trips on my Ark give them much joy,
It's coming closer now. Ahoy!"

"So there's no need to worry at all!" cries Rupert. "What a relief! And how very kind of you, Mr. Noah." Rupert asks Mr. Noah rather timidly if he can wait and take his cuckoo home with him. "Well," says the old man, "that is generally against my rules, but since you have taken so much trouble I may allow it just this once."

Up flies the dove at Noah's sign.
He says, "Go to that Ark of mine!"

Raising his arm he calls loudly and in a few minutes his messenger, the wooden dove, flies to him. "Go to the Ark," he commands. "Tell our guests from Nutwood that the picnic is over and bid seven of our little birds to lead them here."

"I hope our guests enjoyed their fun,
But tell them that the picnic's done."

"Now you must hide, for birds are shy,
And if they're scared, away they'll fly."

When the dove has departed on its mission Mr. Noah takes Rupert behind some bushes. "My little birds don't like strangers," he says. "If they see you too soon they may become shy and fly somewhere else."

So Rupert waits out of sight and before long there is a whirring and creaking of wooden wings as the little dove appears with seven other little birds from the Ark. In their midst is a large shining bird with a huge tail.

The cuckoo's missing from the group,
As swiftly overhead they swoop.

The weathercock cries, "Goodness me,
There's Rupert standing by the tree!"

"That must be the Squire's weathercock!" gasps Rupert. On spying Rupert the weathercock swerves and settles on a tree. "Why, bless my tailfeathers!" it cries in its loud brassy voice. "If it isn't you, Rupert, from Nutwood. I've never seen you so close before. You're bigger than I thought."

"So are you, much bigger than I thought," says Rupert. "But, please, I'm waiting for my cuckoo. Where is it?" "It certainly started from the Ark with us," says the other. So Rupert waits, but the cuckoo does not arrive.

"My wooden cuckoo isn't here,"
Sighs Rupert, "and he's lost, I fear."

Without delay he runs along
And tells the old man what is wrong.

After a while Rupert becomes anxious and he goes to Mr. Noah. "Please, I think something has gone wrong," he says. "You promised that your little guests from Nutwood should come to me.

"When the party of birds arrived the weathercock was among them, but there is no sign of my cuckoo and I'm worried because my clock is no good without it." Mr. Noah looks serious. "What, no cuckoo!" he cries. "I must put that right." And, waving towards the Ark, he shouts some loud orders.

Says Noah with a kindly smile,
"You'll have your cuckoo in a while."

"Though every bird's flown by at last,
My cuckoo hasn't yet come past."

Obeying Mr. Noah's command, all the remaining birds on the Ark fly ashore over Rupert's head and settle on a tree facing the old gentleman, but there is still no cuckoo. Mr. Noah tells them what has happened and for a while there is silence.

Then the messenger dove comes forward. "The cuckoo and the weathercock followed us," it declares, "but we didn't keep an eye on them because they knew the way. The tiny cuckoo must have slipped away unseen."

The dove exclaims, "Well, this could mean
Your cuckoo slipped away unseen."

The animals have searched around
But still the cuckoo isn't found!

Mr. Noah commands every bird at once to search for the missing cuckoo. Then he turns to Rupert. "They cannot search very far," he says. "In fact, except for my messenger dove, they must not go out of sight of the Ark or they might not find their way home."

One by one the birds return without having seen anything of the little truant, and at length Rupert decides he can wait no longer and turns sadly away. "What awful bad luck!" he sighs. "Just when I thought I'd got it back."

To Nutwood Rupert makes a start,
He's feeling very sad at heart.

Soon Rupert stops and gives a shout,
"Hey, Horace, are you still about?"

As Rupert wanders gloomily towards Nutwood he passes the place where he picked blackberries and he calls out to see if Horace the hedgehog is still there. In a few minutes Horace shuffles into sight and listens to the sad story.

"I don't see what you're complaining about," he says grumpily. "Of course, your cuckoo has gone. Don't you remember? All cuckoos go away in the autumn!" "B-but, surely not clock-cuckoos," gasps Rupert. "Ours has never gone before!"

When Rupert's call makes Horace come,
The hedgehog says, "Don't look so glum."

Horace the hedgehog, still grumbling, moves forward. "A cuckoo's a cuckoo even if it does come out of a clock," he says, "and I expect yours has gone with the others. That's the direction they took, towards the sun, and I believe they go to a place called Africa." He turns and disappears into the bushes.

"Yes," Horace grunts, "I told you so,
He's flown to Africa, you know."

"Oh dear, this is worse than ever!" cries Rupert as he hurries back towards the lake and meets some of the animals. "I must find Mr. Noah again now that we know where we may have to look."

"I think," says Rupert, "I should tell
Old Noah where he's gone, as well."

The little bear hears Noah say
That Africa is far away.

Rupert finds Mr. Noah just as the last birds return from their unsuccessful search. "Oh please," he puffs, "Horace says that my cuckoo has probably gone to a place called Africa. D'you know where that is? And can you send your messenger dove to bring him back?"

Mr. Noah looks anxious. "That is a far country and my dove is too busy," he murmurs. Then a little bird chirps, "Cuckoos come back in the spring. Yours is sure to come with them."

"Cheer up, the warmer days will bring
Your cuckoo back again next spring."

Just then, above them in the sky,
The weathercock goes flying by.

Rupert is a little comforted, but not very much. All at once he spies a shining object in the sky. It is the weathercock on its way back to Nutwood. "Hi, you're just the person I want," he calls.

"You don't belong to Mr. Noah, you're free to do as you like. Please, will you fetch my cuckoo back from Africa?" "But I'm not free," says the weathercock importantly. "How do you think the Nutwood people will know which way the wind is blowing if I don't tell them? I must get back to my work. Goodbye."

"I cannot go, so don't ask me,
I have my job to do, you see."

Poor Rupert seems to be no nearer to finding his lost cuckoo. "Mummy will be very unhappy if we have to wait until next spring before our clock can strike again," he says. Mr. Noah too is very sorry and sends his birds up for a final search.

The little birds look everywhere,
But Rupert's cuckoo isn't there.

"Horace may have been wrong when he thought your cuckoo had gone to Africa," he suggests. But the birds, as before, have no success and at length the little bear gives it up and trudges sadly homewards.

"The cuckoo can't be found, I know,
Although they've hunted high and low."

Mrs. Bear sees Rupert coming slowly home. "Well, and what have you found out?" she asks. "Not very much I'm afraid," says Rupert. "I discovered that our cuckoo went to a picnic with Mr. Noah, but nobody has seen it since and Horace thinks it may have gone right away until next spring!"

Says Mrs. Bear, "He's lost, I fear,
But don't upset yourself, my dear."

"Well, well, if it has it can't be helped," sighs Mrs. Bear. "So don't worry too much. It must be nearly four o'clock. Let's have tea." Suddenly Rupert gives a start. "Listen, did you hear what I heard?" he gasps.

Gasps Rupert, "There is no mistake,
That's just the sound that cuckoos make!"

"My cuckoo's back again – hooray!
He didn't really go away!"

The next moment Rupert is capering about in glee. "Why, what ever has come over you all of a sudden?" asks Mrs. Bear mystified. "Didn't you hear?" cries Rupert. "Our cuckoo must have come back!"

Rushing into the cottage he looks at the clock. "Yes, there you are, four o'clock has just struck and it was our cuckoo's voice doing it. Quick, I must make certain." And dragging up a chair he gets level with the clock and opens the little door.

Says Rupert, "Mummy, see the time!
I knew I heard the cuckoo chime!"

Sure enough, as soon as the tiny door is opened the cuckoo pops its head out. "Why, where have you been?" cries Rupert. "I traced you to Mr. Noah's picnic. Then you vanished and Horace thought you had gone to Africa." "Cuckoos from clocks don't go to Africa," declares the other.

When Rupert peeps behind the door
He finds his cuckoo, home once more.

"We're much too busy! No, when I saw you at the picnic I thought you'd be angry with me, so I slipped away. And nobody noticed. And here I am!" Then it pops back, the door shuts, and Rupert is soon having his tea.

At last the family, all three
Sit down and have a lovely tea.

"That cuckoo gave us such a fright,
But now he's home, so that's all right!"

After tea Rupert finds the bird who first set him on the trail. "Will you tell Mr. Noah that my cuckoo came straight home?" he asks. "What a lot of fuss," squawks the bird. "All right. I'll go."

In the village Rupert finds his pals gazing at the Squire's house. "Do look up there," cries Bill Badger. "Nobody has been up to that turret and yet the weathercock is back in its place!" "My cuckoo's back, too," laughs Rupert. And he tells them all the story.

"The weathercock is on its spire,"
Says Rupert. "That will please the Squire."

HERITAGE CLASSICS TO CHERISH FOREVER

LITTLE HOUSE ON THE PRAIRIE

LAURA INGALLS WILDER

THE WIND IN THE WILLOWS

KENNETH GRAHAME
WITH ILLUSTRATIONS BY E. H. SHEPARD

THE BOX OF DELIGHTS

JOHN MASEFIELD

THE HUNDRED AND ONE DALMATIANS

DODIE SMITH

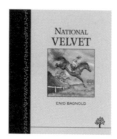

NATIONAL VELVET

ENID BAGNOLD

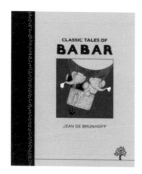

CLASSIC TALES OF BABAR

JEAN DE BRUNHOFF

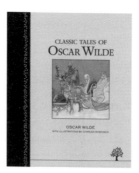

CLASSIC TALES OF OSCAR WILDE

OSCAR WILDE
WITH ILLUSTRATIONS BY CHARLES ROBINSON

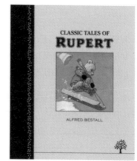

CLASSIC TALES OF RUPERT

ALFRED BESTALL

THE VELVETEEN RABBIT

MARGERY WILLIAMS
WITH ILLUSTRATIONS BY WILLIAM NICHOLSON

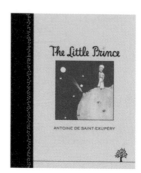

The Little Prince

ANTOINE DE SAINT-EXUPERY

EGMONT PRESS: ETHICAL PUBLISHING

Egmont Press is about turning writers into successful authors and children into passionate readers – producing books that enrich and entertain. As a responsible children's publisher, we go even further, considering the world in which our consumers are growing up.

Safety First
Naturally, all of our books meet legal safety requirements. But we go further than this; every book with play value is tested to the highest standards – if it fails, it's back to the drawing-board.

Made Fairly
We are working to ensure that the workers involved in our supply chain – the people that make our books – are treated with fairness and respect.

Responsible Forestry
We are committed to ensuring all our papers come from environmentally and socially responsible forest sources.

For more information, please visit our website at www.egmont.co.uk/ethical

Egmont is passionate about helping to preserve the world's remaining ancient forests. We only use paper from legal and sustainable forest sources, so we know where every single tree comes from that goes into every paper that makes up every book.

This book is made from paper certified by the Forest Stewardship Council (FSC), an organisation dedicated to promoting responsible management of forest resources. For more information on the FSC, please visit **www.fsc.org**. To learn more about Egmont's sustainable paper policy, please visit **www.egmont.co.uk/ethical**.